ANDY'S   BEST PLAY

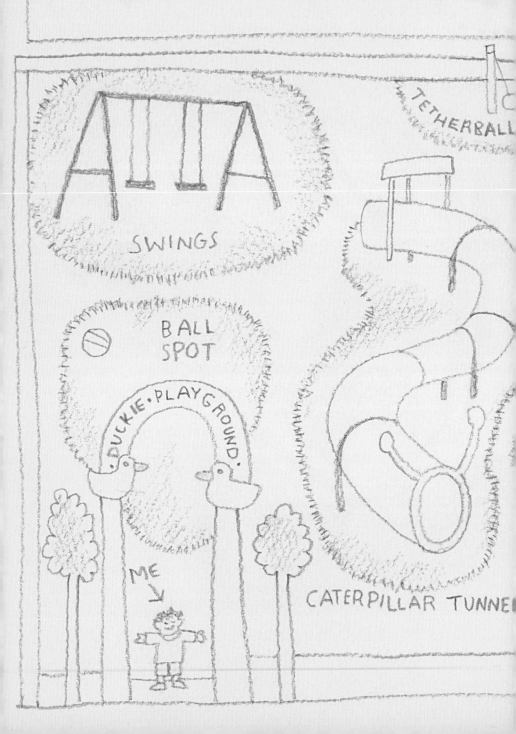

SWINGS

TETHERBALL

BALL
SPOT

· DUCKIE · PLAYGROUND ·

ME

CATERPILLAR TUNNEL

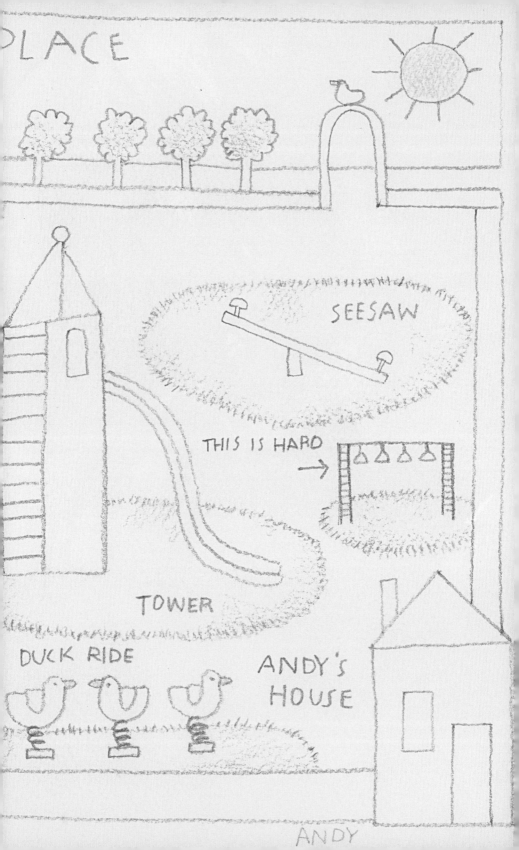

For Judy, Danny, and Mary Grace, with love
—T. deP. and J. L.

And, of course, Jim
—T. deP.

SIMON & SCHUSTER BOOKS FOR YOUNG READERS
An imprint of Simon & Schuster Children's Publishing Division
1230 Avenue of the Americas, New York, New York 10020
Text copyright © 2016 by Tomie dePaola and Jim Lewis
Illustrations copyright © 2016 by Tomie dePaola
All rights reserved, including the right of reproduction in whole or in part in any form.
SIMON & SCHUSTER BOOKS FOR YOUNG READERS is a trademark of Simon & Schuster, Inc.
For information about special discounts for bulk purchases, please contact
Simon & Schuster Special Sales at 1-866-506-1949 or business@simonandschuster.com.
The Simon & Schuster Speakers Bureau can bring authors to your live event.
For more information or to book an event, contact the Simon & Schuster Speakers Bureau
at 1-866-248-3049 or visit our website at www.simonspeakers.com.
Also available in a Simon & Schuster Books for Young Readers paper-over-board edition
Book design by Laurent Linn
The text for this book is set in Minister Std.
The illustrations for this book are rendered in acrylics with colored pencil
on 150lb Fabriano Cold Press 100% rag watercolor paper.
Manufactured in China
0118 SCP
First Simon & Schuster Books for Young Readers paperback edition April 2018
2 4 6 8 10 9 7 5 3 1
The Library of Congress has cataloged the paper-over-board edition as follows:
DePaola, Tomie, 1934– author, illustrator.
When Andy met Sandy / Tomie dePaola. — 1st edition.
pages cm
Summary: When Andy and Sandy first meet at the playground,
they are cautious of one another, but soon find a way to become friends.
ISBN 978-1-4814-4155-1 (paper-over-board) — ISBN 978-1-5344-1372-6 (pbk) —
ISBN 978-1-4814-4156-8 (ebook)
[1. Friendship—Fiction. 2. Playgrounds—Fiction.] I. Title.
PZ7.D439Wf 2016
[E]—dc23
2014047505

When Andy Met Sandy

Tomie dePaola
COWRITTEN WITH Jim Lewis

SIMON & SCHUSTER BOOKS FOR YOUNG READERS
New York   London   Toronto   Sydney   New Delhi

I am Andy.

I am Sandy.

Today I have the playground to myself!

I have never played here before.

She is new here.

Is this
his playground?

Time

to play.

I bet she has lots of friends.

I bet he wants to play
by himself.

If we were friends, she could
help me climb to the top.

If we were friends, he could help me crawl through the tunnel.

I love to swing too.

I love to kick the ball.

Look, a seesaw!

But you cannot ride
a seesaw by yourself.

If we were friends . . .

we could ride the seesaw

together.

Would you like to play?

Yes! Would you?

I am Andy.

I am Sandy.

And we are friends!

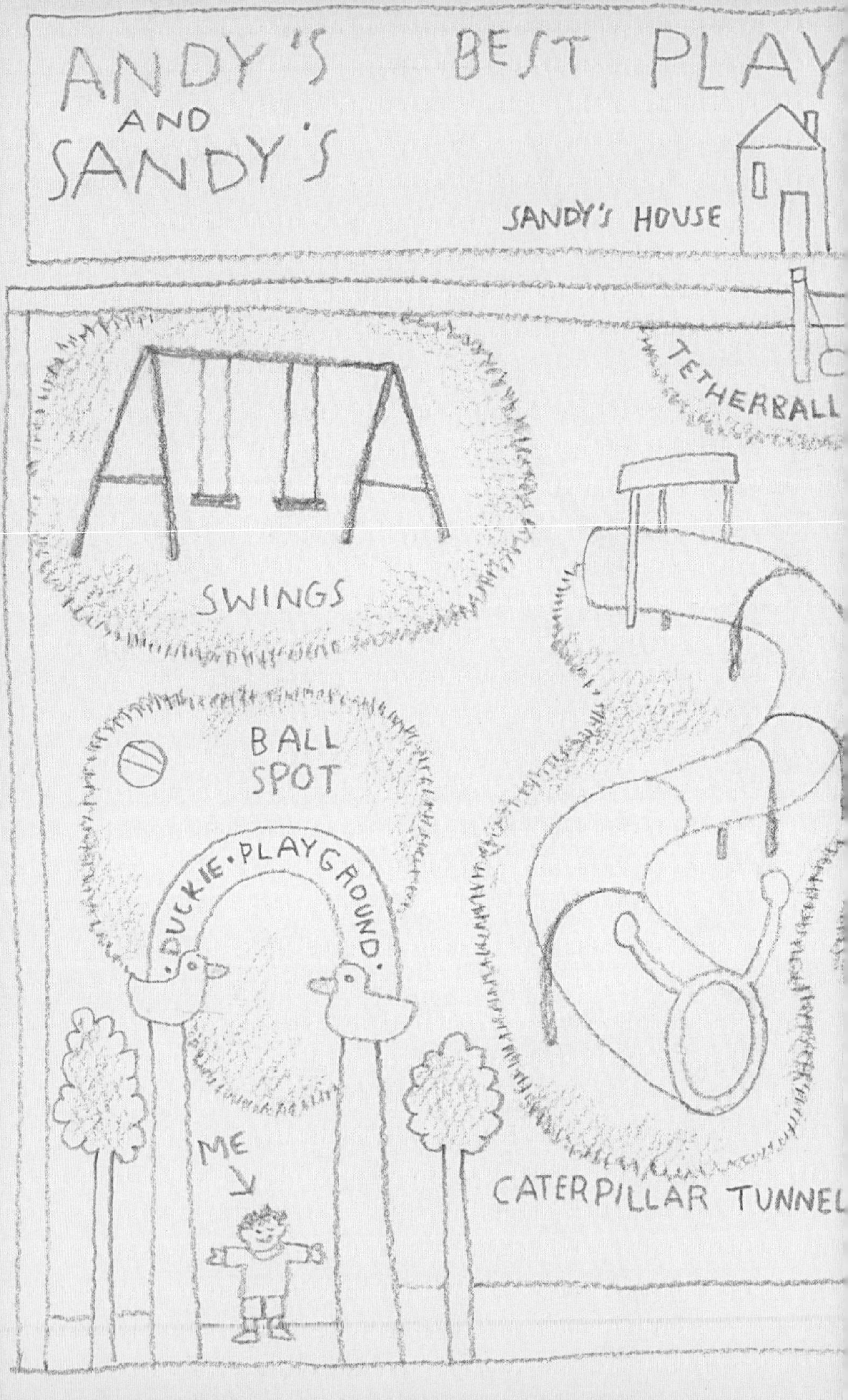

ANDY'S AND SANDY'S BEST PLAY
SANDY'S HOUSE
TETHERBALL
SWINGS
BALL SPOT
DUCKIE • PLAYGROUND •
CATERPILLAR TUNNEL
ME

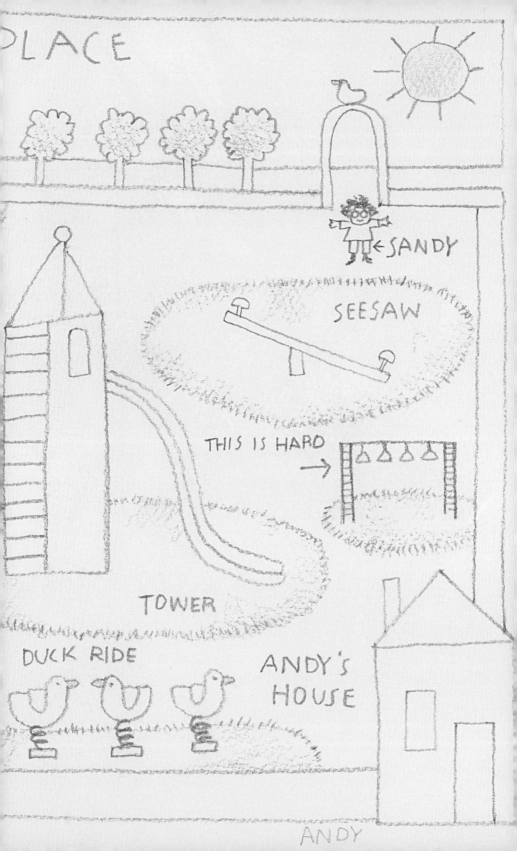